MAX HOWARD

An imprint of Enslow Publishing

WEST **44** BOOKS™

Please visit our website, www.west44books.com.
For a free color catalog of all our high-quality books,
call toll free 1-800-542-2595 or fax 1-877-542-2596.

Cataloging-in-Publication Data

Names: Howard, Max.
Title: The water year / Max Howard.
Description: New York : West 44, 2020. | Series: West 44 YA prose
Identifiers: ISBN 9781538385111 (pbk.) | ISBN 9781538385128
  (library bound) | ISBN 9781538385135 (ebook)
Subjects: LCSH: Emigration and immigration--Juvenile fiction. |
  Immigrants--Juvenile fiction. | Human rights--Juvenile fiction.
Classification: LCC PZ7.1.H693 Wa 2020 | DDC [F]--dc23

First Edition

Published in 2020 by
Enslow Publishing LLC
101 West 23rd Street, Suite #240
New York, NY 10011

Editor: Caitie McAneney
Designer: Seth Hughes

Photo Credits: Cover (dirt) Nopi Mohd Nor/Shutterstock.com.

Printed in the United States of America

CPSIA compliance information: Batch #CW20W44: For further information contact
Enslow Publishing LLC, New York, New York at 1-800-542-2595.

O, yes,
I say it plain,
America never was America to me,
And yet I swear this oath—
America will be!

- Langston Hughes

Chapter 1

Dear Mom,

Lucas Ross is a dung heap with a tongue ring. How is my best friend in love with him?

He gets Doritos stuck in his braces. He clicks his tongue ring against his teeth when other people are talking.

Amy and I usually see eye to eye, but whenever Lucas raises his dumb eyebrows, she laughs. He's always raising his eyebrows. Or else he repeats what you say in a sarcastic voice. He's like a walking meme.

A mean meme.

The worst part is, I hardly ever see Amy anymore.

I miss her.

And you.

Love,
Sophie

"Sophie, you *have* to go to the Sato twins' Fall Bash," Amy says. She swirls her french fries in ketchup. Her boyfriend, Lucas, nuzzles her neck. "Pretty please? I never get to *see* you anymore."

"I don't know. It's weird the party's on a weeknight," Sophie says. She looks down at her lunch. Limp, slimy school pizza slumps on her tray. "I have to go study for my history quiz."

Lucas slides his mouth off Amy's neck. "Uh, Sophie? What's a *weeknight*?"

His voice is serious, but his face is mocking. He clicks his tongue ring against his teeth.

"You know. Like a school night," Sophie says.

"Here's the thing: I don't think *weeknights* exist," Lucas declares.

"He's right," Amy pipes up. "The days of the week are just a social construct. You know. Just something humans made up."

"Weekends are as made-up as Santa Claus," Lucas says. He crunches a fry. "You don't still believe in Santa, do you?"

"I have to go," Sophie says. *Santa might not exist,* she thinks. *But Mr. Orr is a real bear. History quizzes are the worst.*

"Come to the party. There's going to be a bonfire. In the desert! On a full moon," Amy says.

"A full *blood moon*," Lucas adds.

"If you come with us, I'll sleep over Friday *and* Saturday. I'll help you take care of Violet," Amy promises.

"Who's Violet?" says Lucas.

"Sophie's sister," says Amy. "She's in second grade. She's so cute. She's obsessed with that cartoon movie—*Ice Fairies.*"

"That cartoon one about the fairy princesses? With the song about snow—"

Amy and Sophie burst out singing "Here I Am," the hit song from *Ice Fairies.*

Lucas scoffs. "I can't believe you guys like that princess stuff."

"It's about sisters who rescue each other!" Amy says. "And there's no kiss at the end. It's feminist!"

Lucas shrugs. "Is it feminist? Or are they just trying to sell little girls T-shirts?"

"And tutus," Sophie says.

"What?" says Lucas.

"Yeah," says Amy. "They sell tutus, too."

"Violet *only* wears *Ice Fairies* T-shirts and tutus," Sophie says.

"Whatever," says Lucas. "Let's focus. Sophie. You going to the party?" He clicks his tongue ring, making a tick-tock sound.

Yuck. Imagine driving to the party with Lucas and Amy. How long would the car ride be? Would his tongue click the whole way?

But going to the party might be worth it, Sophie muses.

Maybe Amy really would sleep over.

Violet misses Amy, Sophie thought. Amy puts fancy braids in Violet's hair. She teaches her dance moves. She microwaves mint ice cream and calls it "dinner swamp."

But yesterday Violet asked, "Did Amy move away? How come we never see her?"

"OK," Sophie says. "If you sleep over on the weekend, I'll go. The only thing is—what will I tell my dad? He'd never let me go to a party on a school night."

"Just tell your dad that we're going stargazing," Amy says. "You won't be lying. We'll see some stars. The desert's nothing but sky."

Chapter 2

Dear Mom,

After school, I took Violet with me to work at the restaurant. Dad worried. "Keep Violet away from the soup warmer. Soup is at 180 degrees. Maybe you should take her home."

You let me help out at the restaurant. You showed me how to roll silverware in napkins. You taught me how to fill salt shakers.

Back then, Dad made up songs about food. He sang while he flipped burgers. He changed the words to "Old MacDonald Had a Farm." He sang, "Old McDonald's Serves You Horse."

He doesn't sing anymore.

Instead, he worries.

I let Violet put placemats on the tables. Dad snapped at me. "What's your sister doing running around out there? Do you want someone to spill hot coffee all over her?"

I took a quiz online. My emotional intelligence score is off the charts, so I know Dad's not really angry. He's scared. He's been scared ever since you died.

I still don't like it when he yells at me.

Violet liked rolling silverware. She said, "It's like making a napkin taco."

I also let her count cupcakes. I tried to stop her from licking her fingers, but I got distracted.

Love,
Sophie

The phone rings in the restaurant kitchen. Sophie's dad picks it up. "Fresh Ranch Restaurant, Breakfast All Day." He flips pancakes while he listens. "Yep, that's right. All our desserts are from Velez, the best bakery this side of the Mississippi. You want a dozen cupcakes? We should be getting a delivery any minute… can you come by around 4:30 and pick them up?" He hangs up and turns to Sophie.

"Why don't you take Violet out of here and go stock the bakery case? The kitchen's too dangerous. The delivery guy should be coming soon," her dad says.

Sophie blushes. Could he tell she'd been waiting *all day* for the bakery guy to show up?

Rubén Velez has delivered treats to Fresh Ranch for

three years. He used to carry the bakery boxes on his bike. When he turned sixteen, he started driving the green Velez Bakery van.

Whenever she sees Rubén, Sophie tries to shoot pink laser beams of love out of her eyes at him. She wants to melt his heart.

She aims her love lasers at his chest. She can't look him in the eye. It makes her stomach flip.

So far, though, his heart seems unmelted. It seems as frozen as the castle in *Ice Fairies.*

The bell above the door jingles. Is it him? It's him. It's definitely him!

Sophie spies Rubén's wild, brown curls poking up over the huge stack of white bakery boxes. He has great hair. Even Amy agrees. Plus, he always smells like dessert.

When Rubén passes them in the halls at school, Amy teases Sophie. She sniffs loudly and says, "I smell something. Oh, I smell sugar. Ooh, sugar, sugar." ("Ooh, shut up, shut up," Sophie always says.)

Rubén puts the bakery boxes on the counter. He's so close Sophie hears the beats coming out of his earbuds. Sophie trains her love lasers on him. She leans in. He smells like *carlota de limón.* The icebox cake is a Velez specialty.

Sophie breathes in lemony heaven. She opens her mouth. She wants to ask Rubén if he's going to the Sato twins' party.

But he starts texting. He has beautiful, perfect thumbs.

Sophie opens a bakery box. Luckily, she remembered to paint her nails. Her hands look good. Passion pink is definitely her color.

When she opens the box, a cloud of powdered sugar poofs out.

"Ooh, sugar, sugar!" Sophie blurts.

Rubén looks up from his phone.

Blood rushes to Sophie's face. Her ears start to ring. "The cookies. I mean, these are sugar cookies."

Rubén shrugs and goes back to texting.

Who's he texting? Sophie wonders. *Does he have a girlfriend?*

Violet tugs on Sophie's shirt. "Can I help?"

"Here," Sophie says. She opens a box of tres leches cupcakes. "We ordered two dozen cupcakes. Can you count them?"

Violet sticks her finger in a cloud of whipped cream.

"Don't touch," Sophie says.

"I'm not touching. I'm counting," Violet says.

Rubén tucks his phone in his back pocket. "I have little sisters, too," he says. He looks at Violet. "Are you in third grade?"

"Second," says Violet.

"Do you watch Wild Kratts?"

"I prefer *Ice Fairies*." Violet licks whipped cream off the side of her finger.

"Oh yeah, that's Princess Ellie on your T-shirt. I see it now. I'm more of a Princess Arabelle fan, myself." Rubén grins.

"Princess Ellie has magic powers," says Violet. "That's why she's my favorite."

"But Princess Arabelle saves the day!" Rubén says. He raps the counter with his knuckles. "That everything? See you later."

Sophie watches him go. Black jeans, black T-shirt, wild hair.

He scratches the back of his neck when he pushes through the door. There's something so *shy* about his neck.

The bell jingles behind him—and he's gone.

Chapter 3

Dear Mom,

Dad goes to "man camp" with the Desert Rangers three or four times a month. He says it's good for him. Maybe it is.

I don't mind shaking sand out of his sleeping bag when he comes back. I don't mind emptying the cooler. I don't even mind babysitting Violet all weekend.

But I wonder what the Desert Rangers do out there.

Uncle Matt says the point of the Desert Rangers is that I don't have to wonder. "You just get to live your life, safe and sound," he said. "The people who love you are looking out for you."

His voice breaks up when he says "people who love you." He's sad because he and Aunt Rachel are getting divorced. He's so sad that if you try to hug him, he pushes you away. He says, "God! Cut it out! I got to stay focused."

Focused on what?

Dad says Uncle Matt has a long healing journey ahead of him. Maybe man camp is a healing journey. But when Dad comes back from the desert, he looks worried.

He triple-checks the door locks. He bought a motion sensor alarm. Quails keep setting it off in the yard.

Dad even made me memorize the passcode to the gun safe. "Just in case," he said.

Just in case what?

Love,
Sophie

Lucas drives Amy and Sophie to the Sato twins' desert party. Amy keeps one hand on his thigh the whole time. Lucas clicks his tongue ring in time with the turn signal. To Sophie, it feels like a *long* drive.

The Sato twins live far outside of town. At last, Lucas pulls into their winding driveway. Then they bump along a dark, dirt trail behind the Satos' house.

"I heard Rubén Velez is going to be there tonight," Amy says.

"So?" asks Sophie. She doesn't want Lucas to know her business.

"Lucas, don't you think Sophie and Rubén would make a cute couple?"

"I don't really know him," says Lucas. "But I doubt he'll be there tonight. He hates the Sato twins."

"Why?" says Sophie.

"Rubén's a monk. He rejects the party mentality."

"He's not a *monk*," Amy scoffs.

"You ever see him hook up with anybody? You ever see him kick back with a few beers?"

"You don't know what you're talking about. Rubén is totally normal. He hangs out with other people. Older people, maybe," says Amy, hopefully.

"Think what you want," says Lucas. He points toward a flare of light on the horizon. "That's the bonfire, over there."

Lucas turns off the trail. He parks his VW between two tall saguaro cactuses. They walk toward the fire.

The full moon shines brightly. The desert stretches to the mountains. The tall cactuses cast long shadows into the pale sand.

As they near the bonfire, the sounds of laughter, shouts, and drumming grow louder.

"It sounds so primitive," Amy says.

"Humans have been partying for literally forever," Lucas says. "It is our true nature."

♦

Drinking is something Sophie might have done—if her mom were still alive. Whenever Amy drinks or breaks curfew, she gets caught. Amy's mom, Becca, always waits up for her.

When Becca gets mad, she turns red. She shakes her finger. Her Velcro curlers fall out and stick to her pajamas. It's almost cute.

But when Sophie tries to imagine her dad busting her for curfew, it doesn't seem cute. It just seems sad. Her dad would get that tired look on his face. The one that says, *I wasn't supposed to be doing this alone.*

So while Amy drinks, Sophie looks around for Rubén. She doesn't see him. She wanders away from the bonfire. The moonlight makes a silver path on the sand. As she walks, the sounds of the party float away.

Sophie walks toward the mountain. When she reaches a heap of boulders, she stops. She presses her hand against the ancient rock formation.

People have been living in the desert for thousands of years, she muses. *Living here. Dying here. Looking up at the stars and wondering, what are we doing here?*

Something sparkles in the sand. Sophie follows the moonbeam to a spot just beyond the rock formation. She kneels down. She brushes away sand with her fingers.

The patch of sparkle grows. As she brushes sand away, Sophie sees that the glitter formed letters. E-L-L-I-E.

Oh, Sophie thought. *Someone left an* Ice Fairies *T-shirt out here. That's weird.*

But as she sweeps sand away from the shirt, she realizes that whatever she has found is more than a T-shirt.

It's bigger.

More solid.

More human.

Chapter 4

Dear Mom,

Today I found a dead body.

Wait.

That doesn't sound right.

Tonight I went to a party in the desert. I stumbled across—

I don't know who she was.

I don't even know exactly what happened.

Did I scream?

I don't remember.

I saw something sparkling in the sand. I don't know what I thought it was. Maybe crystals?

I brushed away the sand. Something was buried. What did I think it was? Did I think it was treasure?

I had to keep digging.

I looked for a tool. I saw some trash. A couple of torn-up gallon jugs huddled at the base of a prickly pear. I used the handle of a jug to make a shovel.

I scooped sand.

Then I saw the hand—that's when I knew for sure it was a body.

The skin was dried out. Like a mummy's. The fingers were brittle. The nails were painted passion pink. Like mine.

The moon was so bright I could see for miles.

Do I keep digging until I've dug her all the way up, or do I stop and get help now? I wondered.

I dug a little bit more. Maybe I wanted to find her face. I couldn't. Finding the face, digging it up, was taking longer than I thought it should.

Oh, my God, I thought. *Maybe a coyote ran off with her head.*

I didn't want to find a headless woman in the desert. I think that's when I started screaming.

I ran back to the bonfire, yelling, "Call 911!"

Love,
Sophie

Red and blue lights flash. Sophie counts three cop cars. One ambulance.

Two EMTs carry a stretcher into the ambulance. A long, zipped-up bag lies on top of the stretcher. There's a body inside that bag.

A person. A girl. A girl wearing an *Ice Fairies* T-shirt.

Meanwhile, the Sato twins' mom stomps around the dying bonfire. Every time she finds a beer can, she yells. She yells in Japanese, but clearly, she's mad about the beer.

"God," Lucas says. "It's Coors. You'd think finding a dead body would put things in perspective for her."

"Did you see the dead girl's face?" Amy whispers. She snuggles into Sophie's blanket.

Sophie thinks of the girl's *Ice Fairies* T-shirt. Her tiny fingers. Her shriveled skin. Her pink fingernails.

"What did she look like?" asks Amy.

A mummy, Sophie thinks.

But she doesn't say anything. In fact, she hasn't said much since she ran back to the bonfire. "Call 911!" she'd screamed.

Nate Sato ran to get his mom. Nick Sato told everyone to hide the alcohol. When the cops came, Sophie led them out into the desert.

"Bodies dry out pretty fast in the desert," Lucas says. "I bet she looked like a mummy."

Shut up, Lucas, Sophie wants to say, but her throat feels too dry.

"What's that in your hand, Sophie?" says Amy.

Sophie glances down. She's clutching the handle of a plastic jug.

"I found it," Sophie says. She tries to let it go. Her fingers feel frozen.

"Did you find it by the body?" Lucas says. "That's evidence. You should turn it in to the police." He walks over to a police car. He knocks on the window.

The officer opens the car door. When she steps out, Lucas shrinks back. The officer stands over six feet tall. She peers down at Lucas.

"Well?" the officer says.

Lucas points at Sophie. "She's got evidence."

Sophie opens her mouth. No words come out.

"She found this jug thing by the body," Amy says.

The officer snaps on a pair of blue gloves. "I'll take that," she says. She uncurls Sophie's fingers from the jug. The officer clicks her tongue. "Makes me sick."

"What is that, anyway?" says Amy.

"It's a water jug," the officer explains. "Sometimes people leave them in the desert. They're for migrants who are crossing the border. If somebody hadn't come around and cut a hole in this jug, that girl might still be alive."

"She died of thirst?" Amy says.

"That's for the coroner to decide," the officer says. "But I've seen this before. Lots of people die crossing the desert. Adults. Kids. Families. It's dangerous to travel from Mexico to the U.S. on foot." The officer looks at Sophie. "She's the one who found her?"

"Yep," Amy says.

"You take care of your friend," the officer says. "It's not easy to find someone like that. You kids be careful."

Chapter 5

Dear Mom,

I've started sleeping in Violet's bed.

I fall asleep okay, but nightmares wake me up. I dream about Violet. When I wake up, I have to go and check to see if she's breathing.

So it just makes sense to sleep in her bed.

One night I heard you say my name when I was falling asleep.

"Sophie!" you said. It was so real. "Sophie! Get me a glass of water!"

I sat up in bed. I ran down to the kitchen. I poured a glass of water. Then I remembered—you're dead.

You didn't ask for water.

You died of breast cancer four years ago.

Love,
Sophie

Sophie, Amy, and Lucas sit in the back row of the auditorium. As kids file in, Lucas says, "Happy Dead Girl Assembly." Amy laughs. Sophie elbows her, hard.

"Can you tell him to shut up?"

"Huh?" asks Amy.

Principal Lee taps the microphone. "Attention. As you know, a body was found in the desert. Many of you are worried. I want to give you the information you need to move forward. The police don't know the girl's name. They believe she was between twelve and twenty. She may have been traveling from El Salvador."

He flips to a PowerPoint slide: a map of Central America. "El Salvador is south of Guatemala. It is west of Honduras."

He flips to a photo of a woman drinking fizzy water. "We do know she died of thirst. So I don't want any of you to think there's a killer on the loose."

"Except *there is* a killer on the loose," Lucas shouts.

"Shh!" Mr. Orr, the history teacher, turns around. He shakes his head. His white beard wobbles.

Lucas leaps to his feet. "A girl was killed! And you want me to keep quiet?" His tongue ring clicks when he talks, but this time, it doesn't seem so annoying. *This time*, Sophie thinks, *Lucas kind of has a point.*

Principal Lee says, "This young woman died of natural causes."

"*Criminal* causes," Lucas says.

"Someone slashed her water bottle!" Amy shouts.

"She was murdered!" Lucas yells.

"Calm down," says Principal Lee.

"He's right!" someone yells out.

Sophie peers around the dark auditorium. She spots someone standing up, way down in the front row. Someone with wild, curly hair.

Rubén Velez looks small at this distance, but he holds his fist in the air. "This was murder!" he shouts.

"Sit down, all of you," says Principal Lee. "Frankly, I think you all should be more worried about your *own* drinking."

Principal Lee flips to the next slide: a picture of a beer bottle. "The police told me about the desert party. I will not tolerate drinking!"

Rubén doesn't sit down.

Principal Lee flips through the rest of his slides.

Rubén stays standing. He stands there until the bell rings. Still, Rubén doesn't move. He stands there with his fist in the air.

💧

In art class, Sophie rolls her clay into a narrow worm. Amy whispers, "What do you think the dead girl's name was?"

Without thinking, Sophie answers. "Ellie."

"Princess Ellie. That sounds right. Let's hang out after school," Amy says. She pinches a piece of clay into a little heart. She sets it down by Sophie's elbow.

💧

After school, Sophie and Amy stop to gas up the Jeep. While the tank fills, Amy texts Lucas. Sophie cleans up the car.

She opens the hatch. She tidies her dad's "man camp" kit. She folds his jacket. She drains melted ice from the cooler.

But when she picks up the sleeping bag, she freezes.

There, in the back of the Jeep, are a half dozen water jugs—each slashed to bits.

Sophie reaches into the heap of wrecked plastic. It feels like reaching into a pile of bones. She gathers up the plastic in her arms. She dumps it into the gas station trash can.

She checks to see if Amy is watching. Nope. Amy's texting. Good. Sophie's heart pounds.

She doesn't want Amy to see the ruined water jugs. She doesn't want Amy to call Dad a murderer. She doesn't want Amy to see her rolling up the sleeping bag like nothing happened.

Chapter 6

Dear Mom,

Amy wants me to write a play with her. Ms. Shane said she can produce the play spring semester in the black box theater.

I don't know how to write a play, but Amy said we have to. "You found that girl for a reason! Ellie needs you to tell her story."

So we put on *Ice Fairies* to keep Violet busy.

"Our first step is to make an info board," Amy said.

I got out markers and poster board. We spread everything out on the kitchen floor. We lay down on our stomachs.

We got out our phones. We googled. We wrote. We drew.

For the first time in a long time, I felt calm. Maybe it was the squeak of the markers. Maybe it was just being with Amy.

Here are some of the things we wrote on our info board:

- 100 = Number of dead bodies found in the desert every year (just in our county!) Most are people who tried to sneak across the border.

- GUILLERMO + BEATRIZ - Amy's grandparents, immigrated from Puebla, Mexico, in 1969.

- PASSION PINK = We know her nail polish color, but not her name.

- ELLIE = A cartoon fairy princess who traveled far from home, alone; an unidentified body.

- COYOTE = Smuggler hired to sneak people into the U.S. - dangerous!

- MS-13 = Gang that rules El Salvador.

- EL SALVADOR = Ellie's home?

- EIGHT YEARS = Violet's age. Also the age when MS-13 starts making kids work for them.

- MURDER = If you don't want to sell drugs for MS-13, they kill you. Or if you don't want to be a gang member's girlfriend—they kill you. The only option is to RUN FAR AWAY.

- LA BESTIA = The Beast. Also known as The Death Train. When kids run away from gangs in Central America, they sneak on top of freight trains. They ride them north, to the U.S.

- 68,000 = The number of kids who tried to sneak across the U.S. border ALONE, without their parents, in 2014.

- 40 = The number of miles some people walk to cross the desert. 40 miles of desert and mountains. 40 miles without a house or a road or food or water.

After Amy went home, I googled the Desert Rangers. I heard Dad's car in the driveway. I closed my tabs. I cleared my history.

I don't know if you can hear me or not. Dad says you're an angel, but he might just be saying what we want to hear. I don't know what I believe.

I do know I need your help.

Love,
Sophie

"The house looks so clean. Did you mop? Good job, kiddo," says Sophie's dad. He opens three take-out containers from the restaurant. "Fish special tonight."

"What do you do with the Desert Rangers?" she asks.

"You know, nature stuff. Man stuff. Okay, I admit it—birdwatching stuff," her dad says. He cracks open a beer.

"Why do you bring guns?" Sophie says.

"For protection."

"From who?"

"Wildcats."

"Not people?"

"There's nobody out there, honey. Are you worried about me?"

"No."

"After what happened with your mom, it would be normal to worry about something happening to me." He pours his beer into a frosty mug.

"This isn't about Mom!" Sophie says.

"Then what is it about?"

Sophie fills a sippy cup with milk for Violet. Violet still prefers sippy cups. ("They make milk taste better," she says.)

"You lied. There *are* people in the desert."

"OK," her dad says. "Sure. Sometimes."

"So why did you say there weren't people out there?"

"I don't know, Sophie. I've had a long day."

"That girl died out there," Sophie says.

"She shouldn't have been out there."

"Well, she *was*."

"OK," he says.

"She was a migrant girl. She had to be out there. She was crossing the desert."

"She was breaking the law. Don't I tell you not to break

the law?"

"She didn't have to *die*," Sophie says.

"Laws are there to protect us," her dad says. "If the sign at the pool says, 'No Diving,' and you dive anyway, what happens? You crack your head. Law's the law." He takes a big forkful of fish.

"You don't even care," Sophie says. "You don't even care that a girl died. Do you know how much it sucks to die of thirst or heat in the desert? I googled it—"

"Sophie," her dad says, warningly.

"Once you reach the point of heatstroke, it's all over. You get tunnel vision. You wander in the wrong direction. You double up in cramps. You get clumsy. You walk into rock walls. You trip over rocks. You hurt yourself. You throw up, but only blood comes out."

"Sophie! I've had just about enough of this."

"She could've been me!"

"That's where you're wrong. That girl doesn't have anything to do with you and me. Now, go get your sister."

"You don't know anything about it! Maybe she *had* to cross the border. Maybe she had no choice. Maybe she was running away from people who were going to hurt her!"

"You don't know either, Sophie," her dad says, firmly. "You can't know everybody's situation. It's not your job. Your job is simple. Be a good person. Obey the law. Help your family. Now go and get your sister."

Sophie climbs the stairs. She calls Violet's name. But this isn't the end. This is just the beginning.

Chapter 7

Dear Mom,

I've made a decision. It's not sneaking out if I tell YOU where I'm going. So here goes.

Dad is sleeping. Violet is sleeping. But I'm going out to the desert.

I'm going to put water jugs out where I found Ellie. It's the least I can do.

Love,
Sophie

P.S. Before I left, I went through my closet to find some clothes to leave out for migrants. It gets cold in the desert at night. I found my old jean jacket. It smelled like your lily perfume. It was like getting a hug from you. I think it means you're on my side.

Sophie drives into the desert beyond the Sato twins' house. She passes the ashes of the bonfire. She drives toward the mountain.

She pulls up near the mound of boulders. She pops the hatch. She hauls out four gallons of water.

As she walks around the rock formation, she's blinded by a sudden burst of light.

"Who's there?" a man says. "Don't come any closer! I'm armed!"

Sophie drops the water bottles.

They land with a thud.

"Don't shoot!" she says.

Whoever it is lowers the flashlight. The light sweeps over the ground. It illuminates the water jugs at Sophie's feet.

"Oh," the man says. "You're one of us, then?"

"One of who?"

"You're with Human Kind, right?" he says. "You're bringing water for migrants?"

He shines the flashlight on Sophie. "I know you. You're the girl from Fresh Ranch. You're Sophie." He takes a step toward her.

Sophie puts up both her arms, blocking him. "Get away from me!"

"I'm not going to hurt you."

"You threatened to kill me!"

"Sorry about that," he says. "I don't actually have a gun. I just thought you might be one of those Desert Rangers. Those guys are dangerous."

"You still haven't told me who you are," Sophie says.

Her heart pounds. She kneels down, pretending to tie her shoe. She grabs a big rock. Just in case.

"I'm Rubén. I don't know if you remember me. I'm the guy who does your bakery deliveries." He flips the flashlight back on himself.

There, standing in the desert, is Rubén Velez—all curly hair and sparkling brown eyes. "Don't you recognize me?"

"Well, I do *now*," Sophie says. "You shouldn't threaten to shoot people, though."

"I didn't know you were a Human Kind person," he says.

But he did know my name, Sophie thinks. *He remembers me. That's got to be worth something.*

"Want to give me a ride back to base camp?" asks Rubén.

Chapter 8

Dear Mom,

Do you remember what it feels like to be alive? It feels like driving in the dark. The full moon chasing you. Night air flowing through the windows.

The boy you like, the boy who actually knows your name, is sitting beside you. Turning the radio stations. Smelling like he'd been squeezing fresh lemons to make carlota.

He leans close to say, "Turn here!"

His arm brushes against yours.

His arm barely touches you, but suddenly you're aware of your skin. The miracle of it. The tiny cells. The breathing pores. All the things you can feel. You feel them all at once. Hot and cold and velvet. Metal and rose petals. Sunburn and sunlight.

Everything comes together where his arm touches yours.

"Slow down," he says.

But you can't.

Love,
Sophie

There, in the middle of the desert, glowing blue in the moonlight—a Port-A-Potty.

"Welcome to Human Kind base camp," Rubén says. "Park over here."

The whiff of Port-A-Potty isn't very romantic.

But the huge, yellow moon is.

They walk toward a circle of tents. As they walk, Sophie's fingers brush Rubén's.

"Sorry," he says.

They keep walking.

Their shadows twine together. Then their fingers touch again.

Rubén jams his hands in his pockets.

Does he think Sophie's gross? Does he think she was *trying* to hold his hand? The idea makes Sophie nervous. "So, do people live in this camp?" she asks.

"No. They just visit. Volunteers stay a few days at a time. Sometimes a few hours," Rubén explains. "Some volunteers deliver water. Like me. Some go out to do search and rescue. That's why we have a medical tent. Sometimes migrants stay a couple of days, if they're hurt."

As they near camp, a huge black dog bounds up to them. "That's Luna," Rubén says. Luna jumps up on Sophie. She wags her tongue in Sophie's face.

"Luna! Down!" says Rubén.

Luna drops to the ground.

Sophie's never wondered if Rubén liked dogs before. Now he crouches down and rubs Luna's belly. "Luna's nice. Just jumpy," Rubén explains. "She's Betty's dog."

"Who's Betty?" asks Sophie.

She tries to keep her voice normal. But *Betty* sounds like a hot girl. The kind with red lipstick and heavy bangs. Hadn't Amy said that Rubén had "older friends"?

Rubén fishes a cookie from his shirt pocket. Luna snaps it up. "Come on. I'll take you to her tent."

The dog trots after them.

Rubén nods at a group of men sitting by the fire. They're cooking something—it smells like chocolate.

Are they volunteers? Migrants?

Rubén stops outside a big tent with a red cross painted on the side. *It must be a medical tent*, Sophie thinks. Rubén leans inside the tent and calls, "Betty?"

Sophie hears a woman's voice: "Rubén, darling! You were gone so long! I was worried about you!"

Sophie's heart falls.

But then, a tiny, ancient woman steps out of the tent. Her gray hair forms a huge cloud around her face. She gives Rubén a hug. Then she turns to Sophie. She puts her arms around her. Her hug smells like lily perfume. Like Sophie's mom.

"Sophie, this is Betty Fernandez, registered nurse and troublemaker," says Rubén.

"Sophie! At last!" Betty exclaims. "You are quite a find, you know! We find all kinds of wonderful things in the desert. Hummingbirds. Migrants. Hikers. Coyotes. Border Patrol. Wildflowers. Even Desert Rangers. But we hardly *ever* find Sophie, the girl we like from school. Do we, Rubén?"

"Betty!" says Rubén. He kicks at the dirt.

Sophie's jaw drops. Is Rubén embarrassed?

"Excuse me," says Betty. "I mean, the girl we like *from the restaurant!*"

Sophie's heart races. Does Rubén like her back? She tries to keep a poker face, but she can't help smiling.

Rubén stares at his shoes. "I make a lot of deliveries," he says. He turns and goes into the tent. Betty follows, bringing Sophie by the hand.

"Life is too short for this silliness," says Betty. She squeezes Sophie's hand. "Sophie. Tell me the truth. Is there a dance coming up at school?"

"I think so," Sophie says. "It should be homecoming pretty soon." Her eyes dart around the tent. She doesn't want Rubén to think she's looking at him. She spots a table stacked with boxes of supplies: latex gloves, bandages, medicine.

"If Rubén were to ask you to this dance, you'd say yes, wouldn't you?"

"Betty!" says Rubén.

But he's looking at Sophie. He's chewing his lip.

It's Sophie's turn to stare at her shoes. "OK," she says.

Betty claps. "A-ha! I knew it! Now, go on out and sit by the fire. The guys are making cocoa. Cocoa by the fire is an excellent first date. Then next week, go do a water drop-off together. Take Luna with you. By the day of the dance, you'll be good friends. You won't be nervous on the dance floor. Now, scram!"

Chapter 9

Dear Mom,

If you were alive there would be things I wouldn't tell you. Like how Rubén and I skipped class. How we drove out to the camp in the bakery van. Dust clouds rose up around us. We tore through the desert.

Rubén slammed on the brakes to keep from killing a rattlesnake. A dozen donuts flew from the back of the van. They thudded against the windshield. They left frosting kisses on the glass.

More things I wouldn't tell you: how Rubén reached out to help me climb over a boulder. I took his hand. He didn't let go after.

His hand was warm and dry. Our backpacks were full of water jugs. Hand in hand, we sloshed through the desert.

We sat on the edge of a cliff. Our legs dangled against the warm rock. The sky turned pink. The sun grew low in the sky.

I told Rubén how you smelled like lily perfume. How you made Dad sing. How you sat on the floor by my bed and painted your nails passion pink.

You knew if you waited long enough, I'd tell you secrets from my day.

Rubén told me his sixteenth birthday was the best day of his life.

"My mom crossed the desert, on foot, when I was a baby. She carried me on her back," he told me. We gazed out into the valley. The golden light and empty land stretched forever. It was so far to walk!

"We've always lived in the shadows," Rubén said. "But then when I was sixteen, I got DACA. That meant I could get a driver's license."

DACA is a government program. It gives rights to kids who came here illegally with their parents. DACA kids can get jobs. They can get driver's licenses.

"I'm the only person in my family who can drive. Having a legal driver in my family was huge."

On the day I got my license, I drove Violet to violin lessons.

On the day Rubén got his license, he started driving his family around, too. But he also stopped being scared his mom would get arrested for driving his sisters to school or the doctor.

If his mom got arrested, she could get deported.

He's been scared all his life his mom would disappear.

I get that.

We threw pink rocks down into the canyon. The sun set. The sky turned dark blue, then black. We lay back and looked up at the stars. You could say they sparkled. But that wasn't what it felt like. It felt like my whole body was sparkling.

When I got home, I found out Dad didn't have any clean shirts. He stomped around, fussing. I didn't care. I was shining too bright.

Love,
Sophie

"Sophie! You got a zero on your history quiz?" Sophie's dad looks up from his phone.

"Let's focus on this month's books," says Uncle Matt. They're having their monthly "business meeting" in a back booth at Fresh Ranch.

"Uncle Matt, would you like a coffee refill?" Sophie offers.

"Thank you, sweetie," Uncle Matt says.

Sophie gives Uncle Matt her best smile. She knows Uncle Matt misses his wife, Rachel, and their kids. She heard him crying in the restaurant bathroom once. He ran the water and thought no one could hear him.

Now Sophie fills his cup. Steam swirls up from the hot liquid. It looks beautiful.

Everything looks beautiful to Sophie these days. Even the hickeys on her neck. She covers them with one of her mom's lily-scented scarves. She hums while she waits tables.

"Dad, do you need me to work a double shift on Saturday?"

"Don't change the subject," he says.

"Give her a break," says Uncle Matt. "The kid's got a lot on her plate."

Sophie hurries off to refill a customer's coffee. If she can keep her dad off her back until dinner rush, he'll forget all about her history quiz.

She didn't exactly flunk the quiz. She just hadn't taken it. She skipped class. She spent the day with Rubén in the desert. School seemed pointless.

What if she could save someone's life?

♦

Amy wants to see the Human Kind camp. "It's for research. For the play," she says. So they all drive out into the desert—Amy, Lucas, Rubén, and Sophie. It's like a double date.

Rubén's curls glow in the golden afternoon light. Hawks

soar overhead. They barrel down the smooth highway, blasting old country songs.

Amy sings along. Her voice has a fancy trill from choir. Rubén joins in. He sings with a loud country twang.

"You sound like a cowboy!" Sophie giggles. The three of them belt out Johnny Cash as they race down the highway.

When I was just a baby,
my mama told me, "Son,
always be a good boy.
Don't ever play with guns."

In the back seat, Lucas sucks a Tootsie Pop. When his tongue ring clacks against the hard candy, Rubén raises his eyebrows at Sophie. He turns up the volume on Johnny Cash. He bellows the rest of the song.

Sophie covers her mouth to keep from laughing.

♦

At camp, Luna jumps up on Amy. "Hi there, puppy!" Amy coos. "Lucas, get a picture of me—we *have* to put a dog in the play."

"It's strange Betty hasn't come out to say hi," Rubén says. He peeks into her tent. "Betty? You here?"

"I am indeed," Betty says. She knocks open the tent flap with her cane. She hobbles out.

Betty has a bandage on her head. She wears a brace on her knee.

"What happened?" says Sophie.

"I had a fall at home," Betty says. "Tripped on the corner of the rug. But I won't let it keep me from the work. You know all those water jugs you stashed last week? I hear they've all been cut up. Snipped to ribbons. Maybe the Border Patrol did it."

"Or maybe the Desert Rangers," Sophie says. Her throat goes dry saying the words. She hasn't told Rubén her dad is a Desert Ranger. She doesn't know how.

"Who knows?" Betty says. "But you brought some friends today, I see. That's good. You can cover more ground."

"Got to keep ahead of those jug-cutting thugs," Rubén says. He starts filling a frame backpack with water jugs.

"You mean the murderers?" says Lucas. "The desert killers?"

Amy snaps a selfie with Betty.

"I like to think the jug-cutters are just confused," says Betty. "They need to get their heads on straight."

Lucas clicks his tongue ring. "Listen," he says. His voice drips sarcasm. "Do you hear it? It's the world's smallest violin. It's playing the world's saddest song just for people who don't like other people drinking water."

"Oh, my God!" Sophie says.

Rubén hoists up his backpack. He balances the weight of water on his back. "What's the matter?"

"Violin!" says Sophie. "Violin! I'm supposed to pick up Violet from school and take her to violin lessons. She's probably waiting for me right now!"

"It's still playing," Lucas says. "The world's saddest violin is playing for a little rich girl who's late for her violin lesson."

"Shut up, Lucas," says Rubén. He puts his arm around Sophie. Water sloshes in his backpack. "Do you want to go back? We can go back."

When Rubén speaks, everyone else disappears. It feels like Rubén and Sophie are the only two people in the desert. Betty, Amy, Lucas, Luna, the camp—it all blends into sun and wind. It's tempting to let it all fade away. To walk away into the sunlight with Rubén.

Sophie forces herself to think of Violet. She pictures Violet waiting outside Hot Sands Elementary. Violet would stare down the street. She would count every car that passed until she saw the Jeep. "If I leave now, I'll still be super late," Sophie says. "I feel awful."

"My mom will pick up Violet," Amy says. "No problem. I'll just text her."

"Violet will worry," Sophie says. "She won't go with a stranger."

"My mom's not a stranger," Amy says.

Sophie swallows. She looks at Rubén. He adjusts his backpack straps and grins. "Do what you need to do," he says.

"I'll come back for you guys," Sophie says. "I'll get Violet and pick you up later."

◆

Maybe it's the worry making knots in her stomach. Maybe

it's the smooth highway. Maybe it's the cactuses flashing by in the wild orange sunset.

Whatever it is, somehow Sophie doesn't notice she's driving too fast. She doesn't notice the police cruiser, hidden behind a boulder. She doesn't notice until she hears the siren.

Chapter 10

Dear Mom,

WWYMS: also known as, "What Would Your Mom Say?"

This is how most of my conversations with Dad go these days:

You're flunking history.

You're cutting class.

You're forgetting to pick up your sister.

You're getting speeding tickets.

WWYMS?

Oh, and don't forget. You're letting someone—God knows who—suck on your neck. (You think I don't notice? I notice.)

WWYMS?

So. What would you say?

Love,
Sophie

Dear Mom,

I am officially grounded.

Still, today I have to:

- Pick up Violet.
- Run to the bank.
- Get the brakes checked on the Jeep.
- Buy light bulbs and trash bags.
- Get Dad's pills at the pharmacy.
- Pick up table linens at the dry cleaner.

Dad can't ground me. He needs me.

Love,
Sophie

Dear Mom,

Remember how you tried to order cherry pie from Velez Bakery, but they wouldn't make it? Rubén told me why.

His mom crossed the desert when she was seventeen. She had cherry Chapstick in her pocket and a baby on her back.

The coyote who was guiding their group ditched them. He left them all to wander in the desert.

They kept moving. If they stopped, they'd die.

At night, they heard a group of guys out shooting guns.

Were they Border Patrol? Desert Rangers? Nobody knew.

The migrants hid. They lay flat on the bottom of a dry creek bed. Rubén's mom covered his mouth. She prayed he would stay quiet. She got bit by a spider in the dark. Her hand puffed up.

She finally made it to a Greyhound bus station. That's where she met Betty Fernandez. Betty is a nurse. She bandaged Rubén's mom's hand. She helped her find a job.

Later, Betty became one of the first investors in Velez Bakery. If it weren't for serving Velez Bakery treats, Fresh Ranch wouldn't do nearly so well. We're all connected—you, me, Betty, Dad, Rubén, and his mom.

The story has a happy ending. But to this day, Rubén's mom won't mess with cherry flavor. She says it tastes like fear.

Love,
Sophie

Dear Mom,

Amy asked if she could put something about cherry Chapstick in her play. Rubén told her that statistics would make a stronger case. "Look at the data," he said. "The data tells a story."

He gets up early, mixing dough. Baking and frying. At four in the morning, he texted me statistics. Statistics and gifs.

For instance.

- 42% - number of Mexicans living in poverty
- $25 billion - Amount of money Mexicans living in the U.S. sent to help their families back home last year

(GIF of a cat pushing a grocery cart filled with cat food)

His texts give me life.

Love,
Sophie

Dear Mom,

Amy has a LOT to say about hickeys.

She ripped off my scarf in the cafeteria.

"Don't hide your smooch smudge," she said. "A hickey is a letter to the world. It says: 'I was once part of an act of passion... and now I'm just in math class.'" (She got that from Teen Vogue.)

Rubén and I left over 20 gallons of water in the desert yesterday. My back, neck, and legs ache from hauling water in the backpack. Today I limped around the restaurant. I could barely carry a tray.

My whole BODY feels like a letter to the world.

It says LOVE WITHOUT BORDERS.

The customers thought it read THE SERVICE HERE STINKS.

Love,
Sophie

Dear Mom,

I'm going to the homecoming dance.

It's not something I thought I'd be excited about. There always seemed to be more important things to worry about. Cleaning pancake syrup out of Violet's tutu. Waiting tables.

But then I got my dress.

Violet helped me pick it out. It has green sequins. It looks like a mermaid's tail. When I swish around in it, I feel like a laser beam.

Dad is going out with the Desert Rangers the night of the dance. Amy's mom said she'd babysit Violet. (She doesn't know I'm grounded.)

I'll wait til Dad leaves.

Then I'll get dressed.

I should care that I'm lying to Dad.

But I don't.

He cares about me. I know that.

But if I weren't *me*, he wouldn't care whether I lived or died.

What if I had different color skin? Spoke a different language? Was born on the wrong side of the border?

He'd rather cut a water jug than leave me something to drink.

Dad can go out jug-cutting with Uncle Matt. They can shoot their guns in the air. They can pretend they're cowboys.

Just like I can put on my green dress and pretend I'm a laser princess.

Love,
Sophie

Chapter 11

Sophie's green dress sparkles. She spins around the kitchen with Violet like a disco ball. When she and Rubén walk into the ballroom at the Desert Sands Hotel, she feels like starlight.

Rubén is wearing a black T-shirt and black jeans, like usual, but he's added a black sport coat and a new pair of black cowboy boots. When he smiles at Sophie, his eyes twinkle.

As they dance, Sophie's dress shoots green flecks of light everywhere. "Little lasers," Rubén says.

Sophie's green beams hit Nick Sato's white sport coat. They flicker across Mr. Orr's thick white beard.

Sophie laughs.

Who cares about her history quiz?

Sophie's lighting everything up.

Her sparkle dims when she finds Amy. Amy's crying in a bathroom stall. Sophie leans against the stall door. She listens.

"Kendall Coyotl," Amy sniffs. "How could Lucas make out with *Kendall Coyotl*?"

"How could Kendall Coyotl make out with *Lucas*?" Sophie asks. *Oops, she thinks. That was rude.*

Amy doesn't seem to notice.

"I want to go home," Amy moans. "I'm going to call my mom."

"No. Don't go home. Hang out with me and Rubén," Sophie says. "Pretty please?"

"They were slobbering all over each other in the parking lot," Amy sobs. "Behind a cactus. A *skinny* cactus. They were *barely even* hiding."

Just then, Sophie hears Rubén calling from the doorway. "Girls? Excuse me? Can anyone help me find Sophie? It's an emergency."

"I'm coming!" says Sophie.

"Sophie, don't *go!*" Amy wails.

Sophie yanks open the stall door. She drags Amy outside and into the hotel hallway. The pink fringes on Amy's cocktail dress shake.

"Rubén, what's going on?" asks Sophie.

They huddle around Rubén's phone. "I just got a message from Betty. Border Patrol raided the Human Kind camp."

"Is everyone okay?" says Sophie.

"I don't know," Rubén says. "Betty was recording some of it. It was chaotic. I couldn't tell what was happening. Then the recording turned off. Now I can't reach Betty."

Sophie watches Betty's video. She sees flashing lights, hears yelling. As Sophie watches the video, Rihanna's voice floats out from the ballroom: *We found love in a hopeless place.*

Suddenly the screen goes black. The video ends.

We found love in a hopeless place.

Betty has disappeared.

"We have to go see if they're okay," Sophie says. "We have to get to camp."

Sophie's dad has the Jeep, so they take the bakery van. Rubén and Sophie ride up front. Amy perches in the cargo space. Amy's phone dings. She sobs and texts. Mascara runs down her face. She twists the pink fringes on her flapper dress.

"Amy, help yourself to anything you find back there," Rubén offers. He turns onto the highway. "I don't have anything to drink, but there's some chocolate cupcakes."

"OK. I'll drown my sorrows in sugar," Amy says. She pulls a bakery box onto her lap. She passes cupcakes up to Rubén and Sophie.

Sophie eats a cupcake with one hand. She uses Rubén's phone to text Betty.

What's going on?

Is everyone ok?

Is anyone hurt?

Every time Amy's phone dings, Sophie checks to see if Betty's written back. But Betty doesn't reply.

Chapter 12

The camp is a disaster. Trashed tents are ground into the dirt. Water from slashed jugs forms huge, sloppy puddles. Tire tracks crisscross the area.

Boxes of supplies have been smashed. When the wind rises, medical gloves blow like fallen leaves over the camp. Someone has even knocked over the Port-A-Potty. Foul liquid oozes over the ground.

Rubén, Sophie, and Amy scan the area. The moon shines bright. It shows the damage clearly.

"There's no one here," says Rubén.

"It looks like Border Patrol just drove over everything with their trucks," says Sophie. She wipes away a tear.

Rubén takes off his coat. He drapes it over Sophie's shoulders. Then he kicks at the dirt. He hisses out a long, angry sigh.

"Why would they do it?" says Amy. She has tears in her eyes and chocolate all around her mouth.

"Luna!" Rubén calls. "Luna!"

Luna's collar jingles from somewhere in the darkness. Then Luna rushes up to them. She jumps on Rubén. She licks his face.

"It's okay," Rubén says. "You're okay, Luna."

Luna drops to all fours. She runs toward the desert. Then she stops. She cocks her head, looking back at the camp.

"She wants us to follow her," Rubén says.

Luna leads them away from camp. They swish their phone flashlights across the sand. "Look," Sophie says. "Footprints."

"Small footprints," says Rubén, sounding worried.

They follow the footprints. Sophie notices a red light blinking from within the cluster of boulders. What could it be?

They creep closer. They peer into the nest of boulders. There, hiding in the rocks, is a little boy. He wears flashing, light-up sneakers.

Luna darts into the rocks. She snuggles close to the boy. She licks his face.

Rubén calls to the boy in Spanish. He crouches down and speaks to him. Sophie keeps her flashlight pointing straight down. She doesn't want to shine the light in the boy's face. She doesn't want to make him feel afraid.

But she wonders about him. *Who is he? How old is he? Does he know what happened to the people at camp?*

Rubén helps the boy get to his feet. "This is Daniel. He ran away from the camp during the raid," he says.

"What happened to Betty?" says Sophie.

"She got arrested. They pushed her to the ground. They handcuffed her and threw her in the back of a van."

"But she was hurt! Her knee was hurt!" says Sophie.

"And she's old!"

"Betty will be okay. She's a citizen. But Daniel's parents were taken in the raid. Maybe Border Patrol will release them. But my guess is they're in ICE custody by now. That means *las hieleras*."

Sophie sighs. Immigration and Customs Enforcement has a scary reputation.

"What are hieleras?" says Amy.

"It means *icebox*," whispers Sophie. "They lock migrants in cages in freezing-cold rooms. Sometimes for days or weeks. They sleep right on the bare floor."

"Daniel says everyone else—Betty, a couple of other volunteers, and his parents—all got arrested by Border Patrol. They drove over the camp. Daniel ran away in the chaos. Right now, he needs to eat and get to a bus station. He has an aunt and uncle. They live in Phoenix."

"Can he walk okay?" says Sophie.

"He's fine," says Rubén. "Just tired and scared."

🌢

Rubén helps Daniel climb into the front seat of the van. He's so little his feet barely touch the floor.

Amy and Sophie hop in the back with the bakery boxes. Amy offers Daniel a cupcake. When he bites into it, shots ring out.

"Oh, my God," says Amy. "Is that guns? Is someone shooting?

"I think it's the Desert Rangers," Sophie says. "Rubén!

Don't start the car. Don't make a noise. You don't want to attract attention."

"It can't be the Desert Rangers," Rubén said. "Human Kind has a spy in Desert Rangers. He would have said something if the Rangers were meeting up tonight. It's probably just some kids out shooting cactuses."

"But the Desert Rangers *are* meeting up tonight," says Sophie. "I know they are."

"How do you know?" says Rubén.

Sophie swallows.

"He doesn't know?" Amy asks.

"Know what?" asks Rubén.

The car grows quiet. The only sound is Daniel, eating his cupcake hungrily. He licks his fingers. Sophie holds her breath.

"You didn't tell him?" Amy asks.

"I didn't know how," Sophie says.

Another shot rings out. This one sounds closer.

"What?" asks Rubén.

"My dad," Sophie says. "My dad's in the Desert Rangers."

Chapter 13

Rubén doesn't yell. He doesn't swear. In fact, he doesn't say anything.

"I'm sorry," Sophie says.

Rubén shrugs, but he won't look in her eyes.

Sophie's seen Rubén angry before. He raised his fist in protest at the school auditorium. He often spits out words like *jug-cutting thugs* and *cactus Nazis*.

But she's never seen him angry at her.

She leans forward, touches his shoulder. He jerks his arm away.

Another gunshot tears through the night.

In the front seat, Daniel curls up into a little ball.

"How old is he?" asks Sophie.

Rubén is silent.

Amy leans forward. "Anybody want another cupcake?"

Rubén doesn't say anything. Then, suddenly, he throws the car keys onto the dashboard. He opens the door. And he runs out into the desert.

🌢

"Rubén?" Sophie calls.

"Shh!" Amy says. "You don't want to attract attention."

"They could catch him," says Sophie. "The Desert Rangers could catch him."

"What do you think they'd do to him?" asks Amy.

"I don't know," Sophie says.

Daniel starts crying. Sophie pats his back. She takes off Rubén's sport coat. She drapes it over him. She tries to remember Spanish words. "Todo bien. Muy bien," she says.

But it's hard to remember Spanish when she's worried.

Would her dad recognize Rubén? Would he say, "Ah, that's the bakery guy!" when he sees a Latino boy running through the desert? Or would he take aim and shoot?

Dad makes smiley-face pancakes for Violet. He tucks his tie into his shirt to keep it clean when he fries burgers. He listens to '80s pop when he shaves.

Would he really shoot somebody?

"I think they'd call Border Patrol," Sophie says, finally. "If they catch him, they'll call Border Patrol."

"Would that be okay?" says Amy. "Is Rubén a legal citizen?"

"Not exactly," says Sophie.

"Uh-oh," says Amy.

Sophie shoves open the door of the van. "I'm going after him."

Another gunshot cracks through the night.

Amy's phone dings. "Sorry! It's Lucas. I'll put it on silent." She grabs Sophie's arm, squeezes it. "Don't go. It's too dangerous."

"I have to," says Sophie.

"Then I'm going, too," Amy says.

I'm going, too.

When Sophie was afraid to visit her mom in the hospital, Amy said, "I'm going, too." When Sophie was scared to go to the funeral, Amy said, "I'm going, too." Sophie flings her arms around Amy. She hugs her close. For a second it feels like everything will be okay.

"Stay here, Amy. Take care of Daniel."

Headlights flare behind them. A car pulls up. Someone gets out.

"Quick! Lock the doors," says Amy.

Sophie squirms into the driver's seat, preparing to speed away.

"AMY?" a voice calls. "AMY? Are you out here? I'm so sorry!"

Sophie unrolls the window. She can hear Lucas's tongue ring. It clicks against his teeth. The clicks echo against the rocks.

For the first time, she's glad to hear the sound.

Chapter 14

Lucas speaks perfect Spanish. "My mom was born in Colombia," he explains. Lucas sits in the bakery van with Daniel. They eat cupcakes. They play games on Lucas's phone. Lucas even makes Daniel smile.

Amy and Sophie set off into the desert. It's easy to follow Rubén's tracks. The moon shines bright. Plus, they have phone flashlights. Rubén's new cowboy boots leave deep prints in the sand.

When a shot rings out, Amy reaches for Sophie's hand. They move slowly through the desert, holding hands.

"Uh-oh," Amy says.

"What?"

"Tire tracks." She uses her phone flashlight to point out grooves in the sand. "They're too small to be a car. Must be a four-wheeler."

The tracks tell a story. Amy and Sophie read the story as they walk.

Rubén ran into the desert. Someone spotted him. They rode out after him in a four-wheeler. They chased him. He ran until he reached a cliff wall. Then his footprints vanished.

"Do you think whoever was on the ATV took him?"

"It looks like it," says Sophie. She looks up at the moon, as if it could help her. She sighs. They can't call the police. They're miles from the nearest house. They have to do this themselves. "I guess we follow the ATV tracks."

They follow the ATV tracks along the cliff wall. When Amy's flashlight catches Sophie's sequined dress, it sparkles. Jets of green light flash on the midnight cactuses.

They sneak around the cliff wall. They spy the glow of a fire. It illuminates a ring of tents. "That's their camp," Sophie whispers. "Turn off your flashlight."

"I'll go first. You're too sparkly," Amy says. "Do you see that pack rat den, right up near their fire?"

Sophie squints. She studies the desert rats' nest—it's a huge mound of twigs and trash.

"I bet we could sneak up there. We could spy on them and see if they have Rubén," says Amy.

"What if we get caught?" asks Sophie.

"Whatever. We both look super white. They're not going to kill *us*. They might try to *marry* us, but by that time your dad and your uncle can help us."

They get down on all fours and sneak across the sand. "I'm so not dressed for crawling toward a rats' nest," Amy whispers.

"Shh," Sophie says. They crouch behind the pack rat den. They listen. The Desert Rangers are singing.

For a second, Sophie has a wild hope: What if all along, her dad has been going to a desert singing club?

She can't see her dad, but she can hear his voice. He

sounds happy. She smiles. Dad hasn't sounded happy in a long time. Now he's singing along to "Sweet Home Alabama." Somebody's playing it on a Bluetooth speaker.

"Maybe you could just go in and ask your dad about Rubén?" Amy whispers.

"I can't! I'm grounded! Plus, he'd just call Border Patrol anyway."

Sophie peeks up over the mound. Any hopes that her dad is just going to a singing club vanish. A group of guys are, indeed, singing.

But armed men stand guard on each corner of the camp. They wear rifles on their backs. They scan the desert with night-vision goggles.

What if they shoot first and ask questions later?

A rat scurries over Sophie's foot. She bites her lip to keep from crying out.

"Do you see any signs of Rubén?" Amy asks.

Sophie forces herself to look at the scary men with rifles. Two of them stand guard in front of a tent.

"I think he's in that tent," Sophie says. "Two guys are guarding him."

"I got this," Amy says. "My theater training will really come in handy. I'll distract them. You go and get Rubén."

"What will I do once I get him?" says Sophie.

Amy pokes her head up. She studies the scene. "The ATV," she says. "My dad always leaves the keys in his. Just press the starter button. Don't forget to release the parking brake."

Sophie looks past the fire. She spots the ATV. It's

parked just beyond the guarded tent.

"OK," she says.

"You got this," Amy says. "I'm going to go climb up in those rocks near the far edge of the cliff. Wait for my signal, then go!"

Chapter 15

"Help! Help! Help!"

Amy howls from the darkened desert.

Two of the guards rush out toward the sound of Amy's voice.

"Help! They're after me! Oh, my God! There's so many of them! They're gonna kill me!"

"Boys! Let's go!"

Sophie's startled to hear Uncle Matt's voice. She peeks up over the rats' nest. Uncle Matt looks different.

Normally, he slouches like a question mark. Now he's standing straight and tall. He wears a shiny gold badge on his camo jacket. "Roll out!" he shouts. What is he, like, a captain or something?

Uncle Matt marches out into the desert. The rest of the guards follow him. The men around the fire scramble to get ready. Some dive into tents. Others dig in their backpacks. They hurry to get weapons.

Sophie takes a deep breath. Then she stands up, puts her head down, and runs.

She takes the long away around camp. She avoids the

firelight. She runs so fast she stops short when she reaches the tent. She skids, sliding into the sand. She scrambles up and unzips the tent.

Rubén is lying on the floor of the tent. Someone has zip-tied his wrists together. Someone has stuffed a sock in his mouth. When he sees Sophie, his eyes go wide.

She yanks the sock out of his mouth.

"Come on," she says. She grabs him by his armpits and hauls him out of the tent. She dashes toward the ATV.

Please let the keys be in here, Sophie prays. She jumps on the ATV. She presses the starter button. Sure enough, the machine roars to life. *Hot dang, Amy was right!*

Rubén hops up onto the seat behind her. His hands are still bound. He lifts his arms and puts them around Sophie. Once he's secure, they tear out of camp.

"Headlights!" he shouts. Sophie presses buttons. The lights flick on. "Look out! A cactus!" Rubén yells. "Where are we going?"

"Hold on!" Sophie says. Rubén squeezes her rib cage. She turns sharply toward the cliff wall. "We have to pick up Amy."

They blast past the Desert Rangers in a cloud of sand. "I hope they think we're one of them!" Rubén shouts over the roar of the motor.

"Amy's somewhere up in the rocks!" Sophie yells. "Look for her!"

Rubén cranes his neck. Sophie focuses on keeping the ATV steady in the shifting sand. "There she is!"

Sophie brakes. Amy jumps off a boulder. The fringes

on her pink dress flutter as she falls through the air. She lands with a thud on the rack of the ATV.

"Hey! Who is that?" a Ranger shouts.

"They're stealing our ATV!" another Ranger hollers.

"It's the kid! He's escaped!"

And then, Dad's voice— "Sophie? Is that you?"

"Go! Go! Go!" Amy screams. "Full throttle!"

As the ATV speeds off into the night, one of the Desert Rangers whips his rifle off his back. His gold badge shines in the moonlight.

"Matt! Don't shoot!" Dad screams.

Uncle Matt doesn't hear. Or else he doesn't care. He takes aim at the departing vehicle. He fires.

Chapter 16

Dear Mom,

    I've been shot.

            Love,
            Sophie

Chapter 17

Dear Mom,

Uncle Matt is lost in the desert.

He and Dad had a fight. Uncle Matt stormed off. Nobody has heard from him.

Dad won't tell me what they were fighting about. He only says, "Matt broke a gun safety rule. When people aren't safe, I get mad. I get mad when you let Violet use a sharp knife, don't I?"

I know he saw me in the desert.

He just doesn't want to believe it.

I don't want to believe any of it either.

My shoulder hurts. I don't want to go to the hospital. I don't want to get in trouble.

Amy and Rubén watched YouTube videos about treating bullet wounds. The bullet grazed my shoulder. It's not stuck in there. I should be fine. I'm icing it.

I hope Dad doesn't try to make me work in the restaurant today.

There's no way I could carry a tray.

Love,
Sophie

Dear Mom,

The police found the ATV. We ditched it near the Human Kind camp. The cops think it might lead them to Uncle Matt. They're wrong.

Dad knows it.

I know it.

Does he know I know it?

I think he's telling himself he didn't see me in the desert. "You don't have a green dress, do you, Sophie?" he asked.

"No. Why?" I lied.

He went out today to search for Uncle Matt.

His being gone is a relief. I don't have to pretend to feel okay. Every breath hurts. When I inhale, it's like getting shot again.

I try not to breathe.

Violet sat on the floor by my bed all day. She painted her nails. She got pink paint all over her fingers.

She wanted to paint my nails too, but when she touched my hand it hurt so much, I screamed. "Don't call Dad!" I told her.

I want him to find Uncle Matt. I want Uncle Matt to be okay.

But I'm afraid *I'm* not okay.

Love,
Sophie

Dear Mom,

I woke up in the hospital. I haven't been in a hospital since you died. I hate white sheets.

But my shoulder felt much better.

An IV dripped into my wrist. Rubén and Amy sat in plastic chairs. Violet sat on my bed. She painted my fingernails.

"Violet called me," Amy said. "She was worried. We

took you to the hospital."

Violet blew on my fingernail to dry it.

"I haven't been able to reach your dad," Amy said. "It can be hard to get signal out in the desert."

Her voice was neutral. But we all knew what had happened in the desert.

I thought of Uncle Matt. How he cried in the bathroom. How he wore a gold badge on his chest in the desert. You could wander for days without seeing a house. Weeks. Did he have any water with him?

"I'm painting rainbows," Violet said. "I'm painting each of your nails a different rainbow color."

"Betty's out on bail," Rubén said. "She's already fixing up camp. Getting fresh volunteers out there."

"What did they even charge her with?" Amy asked.

I closed my eyes. I liked hearing their voices. They were sweet. But my mind wanted to drift.

"Littering. Trespassing," Ruben said.

"I don't have orange. I'm skipping orange," Violet said.

An idea was growing inside my mouth. There was something I wanted to say. I opened my lips. Tried to speak. Words seemed so far away. Finally, I asked, "What about Daniel?"

"He's okay," Rubén said. "Lucas drove him all the way to Phoenix. He's with his aunt and uncle."

"His parents are still detained," Amy said. "We think they're in an hielera near Tucson, but we can't be sure. I made a million phone calls. So did the Human Kind attorney."

I closed my eyes. I let myself drift. I pictured Daniel, eating cupcakes in the bakery van. What was he doing right now? What would I do if my dad were stuck in an icebox?

"I actually have two shades of violet," Violet said. "Should I do both?"

Two shades of Violet.

I'm so lucky.

Love,
Sophie

Chapter 18

Sophie's phone dings. She opens her eyes. Blinks. Her head feels fuzzy. *Oh, right. I'm in the hospital.* She tries to sit up, but Violet is curled around her, sleeping.

Violet is wearing Sophie's green sequin dress. Violet's tiny. She could swim in Sophie's dress. The emerald gown trails off the side of the bed.

Sophie strains to reach her phone. She tries not to wake up Violet. She checks her texts. Dad has texted:

We found Uncle Matt. He's okay. Ambulance will take him to hospital. I'm headed to Fresh Ranch for lunch rush. Then will visit Matt at hospital.

Rubén has texted, too.

On my way. Need anything?

She even has a text from Betty.

Pulled some strings at the hospital. Nobody will ask questions about your wound. So don't worry. Sometimes it pays to be a nurse!

Sophie leans back into the white pillows. She admires her rainbow nails. She strokes Violet's light brown hair.

A nurse pokes her head into Sophie's room. "We've got a super full house today, honey, so I'm going to pull this curtain shut. Someone else can use the other half of this room." The curtain rattles.

Sophie closes her eyes, relaxing.

Everything is going to be okay.

Right?

◆

The nurse wheels in another patient. They help him into bed. Soon, he starts snoring.

He snores funny. He buzzes like a kazoo. Can they make her share a room with a man? The nurse says it's super temporary. An emergency.

Violet whispers, "That guy snores just like Dad." She snuggles closer to Sophie.

Dad. Sophie pictures him snoring on the sofa. He often falls asleep with a copy of *Restaurant News Weekly* on his face. Sophie usually puts a blanket over him.

Sophie starts to cry. Tears slide down her face. She makes a dam with her fingers. She doesn't want her tears to land in Violet's hair. She doesn't want Violet to know she's sad. How would she explain?

I want things with Dad to go back the way they were. I want Dad to say, "Good job, kiddo," instead of "What would your mom say?"

But I also want to be with Rubén. I want to volunteer with Human Kind.

A few tears escape Sophie's fingers. They drip into Violet's hair. Violet sits up. The sequin dress shoots green light through the white room. "Why are you crying?" asks Violet.

"I'm cryin' 'cause I'm lyin'," Sophie says. She laughs through her tears.

"Lyin' in a hospital bed?" says Violet.

"Yeah," Sophie lies.

Chapter 19

Sophie's roommate buzzes and snores. Then cowboy boots clack across the floor. The floral curtain shakes. "Knock, knock," says Rubén.

He leans into Sophie's side of the room. He tugs on the curtain. "This is a short curtain," he says. "I wouldn't want to take my pants off in here."

"Especially with a roommate," Sophie says. When were they going to move that guy?

"Did you bring tres leches cupcakes?" asks Violet.

"Just for you," Rubén says.

"Sophie's crying," says Violet.

"Violet," says Sophie. "Don't tattle."

Rubén pats Sophie's foot through the sheet. "I don't know *what* you'd have to cry about," he says, grinning.

Sophie smiles. Rubén's sarcasm is unique. Some people are mean-sarcastic. Rubén is fake-happy sarcastic.

Violet leans back in bed. She stretches out in Sophie's green sequin dress. She munches cupcakes. Crumbs fly everywhere.

Rubén squeezes Sophie's big toe. It feels like Morse code.

There's a lot to say. It's hard to know where to start.

Finally, he says, "Human Kind rescued a guy this morning. They found him passed out near one of the water drop-off points. Jug cutters had been there first. He was dehydrated. Delirious. But he's going to be okay."

"Wow," says Sophie.

"He wasn't a migrant. He was a U.S. citizen," Rubén says. He raises his eyebrows.

Could he mean... *Uncle Matt?*

The nurse bustles around on the other side of the curtain. She says, "Sir, can you sit up for me?" The snoring man stops buzzing. "Let me adjust your bed," says the nurse. "There you go. Oh! It looks like you have a visitor. Come on in!"

"Look at my socks," Violet says. She shows off her pink tube socks. She kicks her legs.

The green dress spills off the bed. It brushes the floor. Green light shoots out from under the curtain.

"Look at that sparkle!" says the nurse. "Someone brought a disco ball to the hospital."

Suddenly Sophie hears a familiar voice: *her dad.*

"Matt! Matt! Take a look at that! Doesn't that look like the green dress we saw in the desert?"

Chapter 20

Dear Mom,

When you died, Aunt Rachel tried to comfort me. She said, "Look for pennies. Pennies are signs. They're signs your mom is thinking of you."

I wait tables. Sometimes jerks leave pennies for tips. They drop them in their milkshakes. So the whole Pennies from Heaven idea seemed dumb.

But what happened at the hospital makes me wonder.

There are 500 square miles of desert between us and the border.

I got shot in that desert.

Uncle Matt got lost in that desert.

500 square miles of rattlesnakes, scorpions, hot sun, thirst, and guns.

Yet Uncle Matt and I both survived it.

We even wound up sharing a hospital room.

What does that mean?

Rubén says everything is random. Things seem connected, but they're not.

Amy says things happen for a reason. You just don't always know what that reason is.

I don't know what I think. I know the story is bigger than me and Uncle Matt. Daniel's parents got arrested in the desert. So did Betty. Rubén's mom carried him across the desert. She walked for five days. She crawled on her hands and knees in the night.

Ellie died in the desert. No one ever learned her real name.

Lucas did something nice for a change. He took care of Daniel. (Also: Amy broke up with Lucas.)

Thousands of other people have died in the desert. No one knew their names, either. Their families don't know what happened them.

Their dads don't sit by their beds and cry.

Their uncles don't apologize.

Their boyfriends don't stand there, looking awkward.

Their dads don't blow their noses and say, "Oh, my God. You're the kid from the bakery."

Love,
Sophie

Chapter 21

Two weeks after leaving the hospital, Sophie goes back to work at the restaurant. She has an "okay" from the doctor. She can carry trays. She can drag heavy trash cans into the alley. She's healed.

After the restaurant closes, Sophie and her dad sit in the back booth of the restaurant. They prep silverware and condiments for the next day. They work in silence. Finally her dad clears his throat.

"We need some ground rules," Dad says. "I wish you wouldn't leave water in the desert. It's dangerous."

"I'm going to, though." Sophie combines ketchup bottles. She puts one bottle on top of another. Ketchup drips from one to the other.

"I know. That's why we need ground rules."

"Like what?"

"No more lying."

"So… what if I tell you I'm going to the Human Kind camp?"

Dad wraps a fork and a knife in a paper napkin. He rolls the bundle tight. "If you're going to go, I'm not going to stop you. But we need to make a deal. School comes first."

"Okay," says Sophie.

Dad pulls out his phone. He checks Sophie's grades. "You're flunking history," he says. "What's your plan?"

"Ask Mr. Orr for extra credit?"

"OK. When you're passing history, you can go out to the desert."

Sophie sighs. "That's fair."

"Also, it's too dangerous for you to go at night—"

"But Dad, we have headlamps and—"

"If you go at night, you have to take me with you."

"What?"

"Your uncle and I talked about it. Human Kind saved his life. We owe them. So we're going to guard their camp. Protect them from the Rangers."

"Seriously?"

"Yep," says Dad. "Look, I know you like Rubén. I think he's a nice kid, too, but he shouldn't be in this country. Legally, he's not allowed."

"Sometimes bad laws need to be changed," Sophie says. "Would you support slavery, too, just because it was the law?"

Dad sighs. "I'm trying, Sophie. Why don't you meet me halfway? I think we can both agree that we don't want to see anyone get hurt, so Uncle Matt and I will do our part. We'll keep everyone safe."

"Okay," says Sophie.

"One other thing," says Dad. "I've looked over the books. We can afford a housekeeper. I'm going to hire someone.

I've asked too much of you. You shouldn't have to take care of Violet and the house all by yourself. You deserve to be a kid."

"Thanks, Dad," says Sophie. She wipes the gunky tops of ketchup bottles. She screws on their lids.

"I wish you hadn't grown up so quickly," Dad says. "You've had to act like a grown-up for a long time. Human Kind is a pretty grown-up responsibility, too. Immigration is an issue for adults. Are you sure you don't want to be a kid? Have fun?"

Sophie thinks about Daniel, traveling to Phoenix to stay with relatives he's never met. Or Rubén. He always had to take care of his little sisters so his mom could start her business. Not everybody just gets to be a kid. "I'm sure," Sophie says.

"Promise me you'll try to make room for a *normal* after-school activity."

Sophie thinks for a minute. "Well," she says, "Amy is directing a play."

Chapter 22

Dear Mom,

I never wanted to be an actress, but I like painting sets. I like working in the costume shop. I combed out an old blond wig. It's super long. It was used in Rapunzel in the 1990s.

I braided it into a thick braid. Amy wants Princess Ellie to be a character in her play.

It sounds surreal, but it makes sense.

That movie Violet loves so much... it's about a fairy who leaves home and goes on a journey—and winds up stuck in a forever-winter place. Her sister has to go on a journey to find her and rescue her.

So many migrants go on dangerous journeys. If they are caught by Border Patrol, they are sent to hieleras, or iceboxes. They get stuck in ice castles, just like the fairy princess.

Also, kids who go to my school are literally afraid

of ICE. Not the frozen water, but Immigration and Customs Enforcement. The people who come and take your parents away. Rubén is afraid of ICE. He acts tough. He raises his fist. But I know he's scared.

Amy named her play ICE AT THE BORDER.

Amy wrote the spring play, but I wrote the program. (Mr. Orr said I could get extra credit for history.) Here's part of what I wrote:

This is a play about a hero and a quest.

In books and movies, people go on quests. They travel to strange lands. They face danger. They suffer. They come out the other side. In movies, we call those people heroes.

But it's different in real life.

Real-life people go on quests, too. They risk everything to pursue a better life. They travel to strange lands. They face death. They come out the other side.

But we don't call these people heroes. We call them criminals. Why?

Love,
Sophie

Every year, Fresh Ranch does a huge Mother's Day Special. Sophie's dad buys hundreds of pink helium balloons. He hangs a banner in the parking lot: Moms Eat Free.

Mother's Day Special keeps Sophie and her dad busy. They're so busy they don't have time to feel sad. Rubén stops by after the brunch rush. He ties on an apron. He helps Sophie scrub a mountain of dishes.

"It's funny. Usually I think a lot about my mom on Mother's Day, but today I keep thinking about Ellie's mom. Whoever she is, wherever she is," she tells Rubén.

"I keep thinking about Daniel's mom," says Rubén. "She's back in Mexico now. She's going to try to cross the border again. She wants to get to Daniel."

Sophie scrapes French toast crusts off a plate. "I wish there were a way to celebrate moms you can't just go out to brunch with."

Balloons drift into the steamy kitchen while they work. Pink balloon ribbons tickle their necks. "I have an idea," Rubén says. "Come on. Let's get these balloons together."

They stuff the cargo space in Rubén's van with pink balloons. They cram them in with both hands. The balloons squeak as they pack them in.

"There's a huge roll of bakery twine in the glove box," Rubén says. Sophie uses long pieces of twine to extend the balloons' ribbons. They drive out to Human Kind's new camp.

They haul out masses of balloons. The balloons zip and dive in the wind. Rubén and Sophie clutch handfuls of string. They try to tug the balloons close to them.

Betty Fernandez peeks out of her tent. She shades her eyes. She watches Rubén and Sophie struggle with all the balloons. "Quite a wrestling match," she calls out.

Pink balloons bob in front of Sophie's eyes. She can't see in front of her. All she can hear is the balloons. They thrum against one another.

"It's like walking inside an elephant!" Sophie laughs.

"Or a swarm of bees!" says Rubén.

Sophie looks down. She can just see the heels of Rubén's black cowboy boots. She has to trust him.

He leads her up the steep ridge behind the camp. She holds the balloons steady. He ties the strings around a cactus's crooked arm.

"Okay, let go!" Rubén says.

When Sophie release the balloons, the wind picks up. Dozens of pink balloons soar high into the air—and then stop. The twine holds them. A mass of dancing pink balloons floats in the blue. The balloons mark the spot of the Human Kind camp.

They climb back down to camp.

"Looks beautiful!" Betty says. "You should be able to see that for miles."

Rubén says, "It will give people a stable reference point. Maybe even guide them to camp."

"Let's hope," says Sophie. She hoped the balloons would attract the right people. Not ICE. Not Desert Rangers.

"Let's do more than hope," says Rubén.

They gaze up into the blue sky. Their balloon beacon quivers, beckoning.

WANT TO KEEP READING?

If you liked this book, check out another book
from West 44 Books:

ON THE PLUS SIDE
BY P.A. KURCH

ISBN: 9781538385173

CHAPTER **ONE**

There I was.

Bryan Parker. The smart kid. The quiet kid. The polite kid. The kid who was always asked to help out. Even though I was only seventeen years old, people always said I was going places.

I never got into trouble. I kept to myself. Getting into trouble would've killed me. It would've killed my teachers, too. And my parents! If I ever got in big trouble with them, well...

My parents raised me to responsible. They taught me to admit my mistakes and fix them. I always did that, without fail. My mother was tough on me. She grew up in Korea with a big family. She wanted me to go to college, something that she never got to do. And my dad! He had been to several colleges. Right now, he was even teaching at one.

As a kid, I knew I wanted to be smart. Just like him. So I stuck to school and excelled at everything I did. By seventeen, I applied to college. I was going to make video games someday. I was sure of it, and I was counting down the months until graduation and *life starting*.

But then I'd remember my boring, quiet life in the suburbs. I loved the idea of living in a big city. It was always busy and loud. I could never be bored there.

I was an only child and for good reason. My mom had nine brothers and sisters. My dad had four. They loved the idea of a simpler life. They also loved having their attention all on me—their one child.

My dad's parents were very tough on him growing up. He wasn't allowed to make mistakes. He couldn't get into trouble. So when I was born, he knew that he wanted different for me, and he would tell me this all the time. "Don't ever be afraid to come to me," he'd say. "No matter how much trouble you find yourself in, Bryan."

I know I did well. I stayed out of trouble. I kept a small circle of friends. I made my parents happy.

Sometimes, my mom would get in a mood where she'd yell at me. Maybe my essay for school wasn't quite finished. She was very serious about school. I'd sit there and listen to her lecture me, and then my dad, minutes later, would come to my door. "Don't worry about it," he'd say.

He knew it was okay to take breaks sometimes. He'd invite me into the living room to play video games for a while. My mom would sigh, telling him it was waste of time. My dad would then very gently remind her, "He's only a kid once, Jin."

The argument would end there. "Well. Maybe just for today," she'd say. She knew I needed a break from schoolwork and a quiet life. And that's how it went, for years.

CHECK OUT MORE BOOKS AT:
www.west44books.com

An imprint of Enslow Publishing

WEST 44 BOOKS™

ABOUT THE AUTHOR

Max Howard lives in Wisconsin and is the author of *Fifteen and Change*. Every day, Max tries to remember three things: a) the pen is mightier than the sword b) the first step toward building a better world is having a dream of how things could be different c) the second step is inviting other people to share in that dream.